DISSONANCE

REBECCA JEAN

DEDICATION

To those who find strength in the midst of chaos, and courage in the face of uncertainty. This book is for anyone who has ever felt torn between two worlds, yet persevered to find their own voice. May the journey of dissonance lead to harmony, and may you always remember that even in discord, there is beauty to be found.

ACKNOWLEDGEMENTS

I would like to express my deepest gratitude to everyone who helped bring this book to life. To my family and friends, your unwavering support and understanding have been my constant anchor throughout this journey.

To the readers, thank you for embarking on this adventure with me. I hope Amy's journey, filled with internal struggles and haunting questions, resonates with you as deeply as it has with me. This book is as much yours as it is mine, and I am truly grateful for your presence in this story.

May you find meaning in the dissonance.

CHAPTER 01

SAY HI TO HIM

The crisp of the leaves on the walkway added a natural aura to the overall approaching Autumn. It was a sign of better nights, with warmer days, but that did not seem to affect the lively mood of Amy. Her curls landed soft on her waist, and her high cheekbones added more attraction and attention to her face than she wanted.

Amy Winters was sitting quietly by her bedroom window with a blank and cold expression, much resembling the cold winds outside. Her frail arms were wrapped around her equally frail body, and her short height frame could adjust in the armchair entirely without needing any space for her legs. She watched the sky with her deep-set eyes, a glint of hopelessness in them and an unspeakable sadness. Was it chronic depression or mere fatigue? One couldn't tell, but for sure, what one could tell was the underlying chaos, as though there were loud thoughts and ideas being exchanged inside that curled hair head.

She ignored the usual noise of the kids and the daily monotonous sounds of people existing near her. Amy Winters had zoned out to some place, to probably a different zone or a dimension. She pressed her hands against her temples, feeling the throb of a familiar headache forming. It always came when she thought about him.

Her gaze softened for a while, the corner of her lips etched ever so slightly, as though in response to something being said – but there was no one in her room except for herself. She looked at the corner where she had her cupboard and stared at it for a good period of time. It was spotlessly clean, but there was something she had her eyes on. Or was it someone?

Amy was the only child of Marie and Nick Winters, but with that came the burden of outperforming in academics and sports, both of which were too hard on poor Amy. Her physical structure did not allow her to be rigorous with sports as much as she wanted to, and her wild and vivid thoughts were often frowned upon by her teachers. There was once an assignment that required multiple roles, meaning that a pupil had to choose to pick two opposite roles, write a script, and perform in the class. It was a part of the activity that they called the development of children's mental health. Amy had singlehandedly prepared a brilliant script for a psychiatrist and a patient. She had used the teacher's chair as a psychiatrist. When it was time to reverse the roles, the kids could almost swear that they had seen Amy as a psychiatrist and a patient at the same time. When asked, Amy shrugged and said that those were props to enhance the effect. She had asked her patient how she was feeling and whether she was taking her medications on time. After this, the patient begins with the daily routine and is abruptly interrupted by another personality, another person in the same person, or one of the others.

The class and the teacher were spellbound at the marvelous performance and had clapped till their hands were sore. Amy had changed voices and positions to suit the magnitude of the personality she was playing. It was convincing to the point where some kids desperately wanted to use the restroom. Amy had the climax at the end: one of the patients kills the psychiatrist, and the others help her escape. She had brilliantly executed it all in a room with graceful ease.

With a dull thudding headache that was minor, Amy looked at the sky again with a more meaningful expression than before. Her face had a different look, as though it was not Amy but someone else.

"There you are," A voice broke the trance.

"Amy?" her mother called out again, but no response.

A strong breeze ruffled the leaves outside her window. But there was an eerie silence in the room.

"Fine. I will just sit here. You don't mind my company, do you?" there was a strong hint of disappointment in the way her mother had put her question.

Mrs. Winters had a staunch personality, with an air of arrogance, as some people put it, but she refuted that claim. What seemed like arrogance was merely a strict code of conduct that she had to apply in her life to protect herself and her only child, Amy. Being a devoted catholic, she believed in the basic principles of what God instructed her to believe in; they were simple: no alcohol or sex outside marriage and that the Son died on the cross for the sins of mankind.

Amy had blasphemously rebelled against the idea, saying that the concept of the trinity wasn't there until more than a century after Christ and that it was nothing but a fabrication of the Christian emperors and kings for their own motives. A slap on the face was the only answer Mrs. Winters could give to her daughter.

"You have no respect for the salvation, you…." she had gritted teeth, mostly out of hopelessness and the sheer humiliation she felt — her child was speaking against the beliefs she had endorsed in her mind and soul.

"I don't believe that God ever had a son," Amy said with a straight face.

"Seek forgiveness," Mrs. Winter repeated herself.

"There is a God, but He begets not nor is He begotten." Amy persisted.

Mrs. Winters felt utterly helpless against her very own blood.

It was years and years of resentment that Amy had built in her. Her mother had surrendered but never really managed to break down the ice barrier Amy had. Living under the same roof, they were like two strangers. Mrs. Winters longed for a warm hug or a word of affection from her distant daughter, but all she had was a stiff and cold human being ignoring her existence.

Amy had long learned to remain silent.

"Do you want some coffee?" She asked her daughter.

Silence.

Mrs. Winters shook her head and opened her Bible to read. She already had a coffee mug in her hand. Her bonny hands and skinny figure looked like a ghost in the corner of the room. A cosy sofa was placed to add comfort for the resident of the room, but it was seldom used by Amy. She preferred sitting by the window. Not once had she turned to look at her mother.

With a deep breath, she opened the first passage and began to read.

"You are disturbing him," Amy said in a grave tone. Her voice broke the silence and lifted that heavy invisible fog of discomfort in the room.

Mrs. Winters almost spilled her coffee. Where did that voice come from? Amy?

"Jesus Christ, Amy, you scared me," she put the mug down on the table where there were some magazines carelessly resting on dust. They were Teen Love with all sorts of immoralities, as Mrs Winters put it. She gazed at the front page, which had a young girl on the cover. Her thighs were visible, and so were her other body parts, except for the breasts and vagina.

"Good Lord, Amy," she sighed.

Mrs. Winters was entirely distracted by the sight of that God-forbidden girl on the front cover; the line that Amy said to her escaped her mind.

"Impeccable timing, you are late," Amy said again.

"Oh, no, this is my usual time of having coffee and reading the Bible. I just didn't feel like doing it today all by myself, so here I am in your room, with you, I mean." Mrs. Winters said. She could feel the urge to speak more, to do more, and to, perhaps, hold her daughter for a gesture of affection, but she withdrew and abstained from those thoughts. Amy didn't like that.

"Do you have a sore throat?" Mrs. Winters couldn't help but ask. The fact that her daughter had spoken was a miracle. But what had she said, something about disturbing him? Him?

"But if it is by the Spirit of God that I drive out demons, then the kingdom of God has come upon you," Amy said with her back to Mrs. Winters.

It took a while for Mrs. Winters to process what was going on. Amy had just read the exact verse from the Bible that was in front of Mrs. Winters. It was as though someone had dictated Amy to recite that verse.

Mrs. Winters stared at Amy horrified, and was too shocked to react. Her breathing and pulse had increased; it was as though the ground beneath her feet had been removed, and she was falling down into a bottomless hellhole. She could feel perspiration forming on her forehead and armpits. Her mind sped off like a racehorse with all sorts of thoughts and questions twirling and twisting her stomach in a knot.

The coffee mug spilled and fell on the floor. Splatters of coffee were on her clothes and the wall next to the sofa. Mrs. Winters swore on the holy Mary that she had not moved an inch. She had absolutely not even touched that mug, so how…

"In the name of God…" Mrs. Winters muttered to herself.

She thought she would have to clean the mess herself since Amy was too occupied with her thoughts and couldn't be bothered with any responsibility.

Mrs. Winters rubbed her forehead and looked in the direction of Amy, who was facing the sky. She had now turned to look blankly at Mrs. Winters.

Mother Mary…

Again, Mrs. Winters could swear on the Bible itself that there was not the slightest sound of movement of Amy shifting position. In order to turn all the way back, she would have to stand on the floor and then turn, and then seat herself, facing Mrs. Winters; all of that required the leather chair producing that embarrassing farting sound and that creaking of the planks, or the gentle thud of Amy's weight on the floor. There was nothing but that eerie silence in the room ever since Amy had spoken those words and had recited the verse. Mrs. Winters's face had gone pale. She clung to the Bible and placed it on her chest as though it was a shield from her daughter.

Amy looked at her mother with a slightly tilted head and a blank expression without blinking her eyes for a second.

"I am sorry; I will clean it." Mrs. Winters said in a trembling voice. She rushed to the kitchen and let the water run down the sink. She dipped her face in the water and tried to refresh her senses.

You are growing old, Stella. That's all. You are hearing voices and seeing things that are not real. This is nothing but getting older.

Mrs. Winters picked up a pail of water and the mop rag, and with a steady pace, she proceeded towards Amy's room. Her apartment was cozy and comfortable in the evenings when she prayed and asked God to forgive her daughter, for she knew not. Cautious steps and a speeding heart, Mrs. Winters reached the door of Amy's room. She knew she had not closed it behind her. She was too scared, terrified, and all the words in every language to describe the terror she had felt in the presence of the child she had raised herself.

Maybe Amy closed it. She keeps it closed, doesn't she…?

Mrs. Winters turned the knob and entered the room. It was awfully cold, even though the windows were shut. Amy was still sitting in the same position, staring blankly at the very same spot where Mrs. Winters was once seated. Amy's gaze was fixed at a spot that was parallel to her eye level, as though she was looking at someone, and not something. Amy didn't blink for a second.

Mrs. Winters ignored her estranged daughter and thought maybe it was one of her tantrums. She cleaned the floor and picked up the pieces of the broken mug. She turned to look at Amy, who was nodding her head in agreement, with that same cold, death stare on that same eye level.

Mrs. Winters could feel that ice-cold run in her bones. She picked up the pieces, the pail, and left the room. This time, she made sure to close it behind her. For the first time in her life, she wanted her daughter to stay away from her. It was not her daughter. She could stand in front of the cross and swear by the Bible, by the Rosary, and by Christ; that was not Amy.

And then, like the bells in the church or the ones in a Hindu temple, it struck her; there was something Amy had said to her.

You are disturbing him.

Was it him, who had spilled the coffee and made me get off that sofa? Was it him who recited the…him? An angel? A guardian angel? No. Then? The devil. Lucifer. Satan.

CHAPTER 02

IS IT A DREAM OR A

TWISTED REALITY?

The dawn of the next day had been a slow, daunting, and lingering one, as though careful to evade the night's darkness and give way to a full, bright day. Mrs. Winters had not been able to sleep properly for the nights after that time with her daughter. Years of her service to the church had taught her one staunch lesson out of the many: that the devil is real, very, very real, and a very real adversary of all men. He tricks and manipulates people so that they can perform acts of blasphemy. What she had witnessed in her daughter's room yesterday was an example of what the devil was capable of, but to entirely label the episode as Satan's handiwork was a far-fetched idea. Mrs. Winters needed some coffee in her system to kick-start her brain into the thinking mode.

She got off the bed, made the bed, washed herself in the bathroom, and combed her hair. These were years and years of rituals that she had diligently followed without any exceptions. As soon as she opened the door to her room, an air of rusty blood engulfed her. She choked and coughed.

"Good, God, Amy, what have you been cooking?"

There was no answer from Amy. She had been acting quite weirdly, and though that was not unusual for Mrs. Winters, she could still feel an uneasiness with her daughter. It wasn't something she could exactly put her finger on, but there was a certain heaviness in the air those days. The days after, she had spilled the coffee and felt him.

Mrs. Winters shuddered at the thought. Those dead eyes staring into the same spot she was sitting in, and that sudden change of temperature in the room, and the coffee spilling itself, and the biblical words coming from her darling daughter's mouth…Mrs. Winters poured herself some coffee. Her nerves could hardly handle real life without the caffeine hit – now to deal with someone, or something paranormal was another level of strength she needed.

"Amy?" the stench was getting nastier and nastier with every moment. Mrs. Winters opened the windows for ventilation and called out to her daughter again. There was no sound from her room; the door was closed shut as if to bar her or anyone from entering his site. Why the fuck was she addressing or acknowledging him as a real being. And who was this him, anyway? She cursed herself for thinking that a ghost or a spirit had haunted her daughter. It was absurd.

"Amy? Are you up?" she called again.

No answer.

Amy was an early riser. She would get ready and sketch in her room all day and sometimes till the late hours of the night. With the outside world, she had bare minimum contact. An introvert at heart, Amy liked to paint, draw, and sketch, which she used as a way to cope with her feelings. She had never had any strong social bond with any human, not even her mother. Much of that distance had more to do with her father.

Mrs. Winters took careful steps and approached Amy's room. She took a deep breath and turned the knob. The door creaked slightly and opened. Inside was darkness. Absolute darkness. It was as if Mrs. Winters had been transported into one of those extraterrestrial lands where there was neither the moon nor the sun to illuminate the surroundings.

Good Lord, she prayed under her breath.

In the darkness, she used her memory and senses to reach for the window. One step at a time. The floor seemed squishy, and it wasn't exactly a pillow when Mrs. Winters thought she had hit something with her toe. There was a soft side to it, and yet there was a hard, stiff side, too, as though there were bones.

Bones…

Mrs. Winters could feel the air around her getting tense, and though she could run outside the room and not look back, her teenage daughter was asleep in the bed, unaware of the stink in the house or some sort of bones and flesh on her floor. Mrs. Winters felt a wave of terror that crippled her and made her feel as though this was all a dream, and she would wake up any minute to see that her daughter was not a demon after all. She would do anything to make it all disappear and have the old version of her daughter back. Distant? Yes, but demonic? Fuck no.

She couldn't bear the thought of leaving Amy in the room, so she took another step, which landed her in something wet and sticky. The odor of rust was very strong. Gathering all the courage Mrs. Winters had in her, she reached for the curtains and pulled them to a side. To her horror, the windows had been painted red. The rays of sun peeked through the window but with a red hue that was diabolical at the very least. She gaped, exhaled, and then turned her head to take a look at the room. Her daughter's hands were covered in blood, and the squishy bony that she had hit earlier was a dead cat. From its expression, Mrs. Winters could tell that the poor thing had been strangled after being tortured. Patches of fur were missing from its body, and the figure was gutted with all the intestines spread all over the floor. As if it wasn't enough, Mrs. Winters's gaze followed the blood trail that led to Amy's bed. Her sleeping posture was odd for any human being; she was lying like a spider on all fours, but her head was twisted on the left side. That was when Mrs. Winters saw her daughter's dark eyes staring at her. Amy's mouth was smeared in blood.

Mrs. Winters stared in utmost horror at those dead eyes; it was the same expression Amy had worn last night when she was staring at the sofa. On the left corner of the room, there was another pile of blood and chunks of flesh, which caught Mrs. Winters's attention.

"What is it, Stella… Ich singe überhaupt nicht gut." A throaty growl addressed her. The voice felt like it came from a deep, dark well with all sorts of demonic activities down under.

Her breathing grew rapid as she stood still and stared at that heap of blood. She did not dare to look at Amy, who was staring at her mother. A crooked smile formed at the corners of Amy's lips. The dreaded look on her mother's face seemed to amuse her.

"Stella…Under the water under the sea… *Ich singe überhaupt*," the guttural sound that formed the word *Stella* came from Amy.

It was mocking Mrs. Winters with a nursery rhyme that Amy's father sang for her when she was an infant.

"Amy," Mrs. Winters whispered with a shaky voice, knowing full well that whatever was lying on the bed was not Amy.

"Oh, no, Amy is asleep with us," the voice came again.

"Isn't she, Patricia?" The evil demon spoke and rose from the bed.

Mrs. Winters calculated the time and steps it would take for her to dash out of the room, but then she looked at her child, her daughter, her blood. Her legs did not obey the screaming of her brain; she stood there frozen with wobbling knees and a thumping heart.

Amy sat with her legs crossed, staring at her mother. A strong smell of urine hit Mrs. Winters, and then she realized that her daughter had urinated on the bed. With a smile. Wide smile. Ear to ear.

Fuck…

"Stella, you poor thing," A voice of a stern woman with a Scottish accent said, "Now, must you go through all the trouble of cleaning and washing all this? I know the others can be messy. I shall do it for you, the cleaning part, so you can rest your nerves." Amy had folded her palms on her lap and spoke with diligence and grace. If it were not for the blood on her face and the disheveled state she was in, she could have passed for a royal queen or a princess with her air of grace and manners.

Amy rose from the bed and walked in a very composed manner when suddenly she changed her demeanor and hunched forward. She took steps that were not forward but sideways and tilted her head to look at Mrs. Winters again.

"Throw away that water. I am warning you," the sound was harsh. Mrs. Winters could not bring herself to call it a voice; it sounded more like a trumpet of death, or immense agony, or something far worse than those two put together.

Mrs. Winters fainted and dropped on the floor.

It took her a while to regain her consciousness. She was lying in her bed. The house smelled of a citrus and fruity scent, typical of Amy to light candles for her art. She liked to keep the place spotlessly clean, but on days, she could be messy. Her dim humming was audible from where she was doing some of the chores.

What on earth…Did I dream it?

Amy had prepared breakfast and set it on the table. Drowsily, Mrs. Winters reached the dining room and was stunned. There was no scent of rust or blood in the air. Amy looked like she had taken a bath, and had applied her vanilla lotion, too. The kitchen counter was clean; the curtains were drawn just enough to let some sunlight into the room. Mrs. Winters shuddered and flinched at the thought of Amy's room. The horrors that had taken place, the dead cat, the piling of blood and flesh, human flesh? Fuck, no, please…. what was it, then? Another animal? And…Amy…those eyes…

"Amy?" Mrs. Winters called out.

No answer. However, she was in the listening range.

"Hello?" Mrs. Winters said.

"Yes?" Amy turned to look at her mother with a straight face. It was mildly strange that she did not respond to her name or show any emotion; it happened at times. That was expected of her; she rarely smiled or had any hint of warmth on her face.

"Um, did you, um, sleep well?" Mrs. Winters asked, cautiously staring at her expressions for any guilt or concealment.

"Yes," she replied and resumed her paintbrush. She was painting something and seemed genuinely oblivious to what Mrs. Winters was trying to process.

The dead cat… Charlie…

"Honey, where is Charlie? I didn't see him." Mrs. Winters asked about the orange stray that they fed daily. He was tame enough to let both Amy and Mrs. Winters pet him but not enough to be an indoor cat. So they fed him and let him roam around the alley.

"I fed him early morning," Amy replied without looking up. Her voice was awfully calm, and she had a different way of talking, a Scottish accent that Mrs. Winters barely noticed - her head was vertigo of clattering thoughts; she did not pay much attention to it. A lock of hair came loose from the braid she had carelessly made. She tossed it with her paintbrush with steady hands.

Is this all normal? Am I hallucinating?

"Did you make your bed?" Mrs. Winters could feel her bowels getting loose at the thought of what she had seen inside Amy's bedroom.

"Yes," Amy nodded again without looking up at her mother.

"Okay, I will take your laundry." Mrs. Winters said as an excuse to enter Amy's room.

"Okay," Amy replied.

Mrs. Winters just had to see what was the current state of the room that was a slaughter house just a while ago, when she had passed out. She could feel her pulse drumming in her temples, but she just had to. She knew that the daughter she had known and raised was not the same, or at least, had some dark entity with her, and in the room, too, but she had to see the room regardless of all that. It was not curiosity. It was confirmation of her sanity. She took steps towards the room and turned to see Amy, half-expecting her to walk sideways and drag her to the room, screaming her name in that same guttural voice. However, Amy seemed absolutely nonchalant; she used colors in her painting to portray the imagery she had in her mind.

Mrs. Winters had almost reached the door.

She prayed to God and touched the knob. It felt oddly cold.

Fuck…No, Stella, run….

She turned the knob and looked at Amy. She did not even look at Mrs. Winters. Painting and humming gently.

The door opened slowly. Mrs. Winters used gentle force to push it, as though she took time to embrace or acknowledge dead bodies inside. Dead animals, idols, what else?

There was a bright light in the room. The curtains were tucked into their corners, letting all the sunlight inside. The floor was sparkling, the bedsheets were smelling of detergent, and there was not a drop of blood anywhere on the floor. Mrs. Winters frowned and stepped inside, reflexively, turning to see if Amy had crawled like a spider and asked her to fuck herself, but she hadn't. She was stroking her brush on the canvas. Gentle humming, too.

Mrs. Winters looked around, especially at the left corner of the room, for that pile of…. *nothing?*

I am dreaming.

Was that a dream, or is this a dream? Mrs. Winters dreadfully pinched her palm, which hurt. It was a relief to be in this reality, where her daughter was the normal version of a human being who does not have dead animals and dead people in her room with blood all over her hands and mouth. That was too much to deal with; even as a devoted catholic, she found it hard to fight the devil in her daughter.

Clouded with her thoughts, she had not realized that in the distance, she had felt someone approaching her. The thudding of the footsteps did not match with the pace of Amy. Someone had now reached her and was just behind her. Mrs. Winters swallowed and felt her mouth as dry as her sex life. She gently turned around to see Amy looking at her.

"Excuse me, I need more paints." She brushed past Mrs. Winters, picked up some bottles, and then returned to the dining room.

It was a relief to see Amy not being…. demonic. Mrs. Winters shrugged the thoughts and went to the kitchen for some coffee. She poured herself a cup and sat on the sofa across from Amy. She refrained from any conversation because she knew Amy disliked it. She silently sipped on her coffee and tried to push away all that had suddenly happened to her and her daughter.

Once Amy was done, she stared at the painting. A frown crossed her face, indicating her dissatisfaction with what the painting looked like. Amy sat and said nothing for a long time.

Mrs. Winters casually looked at her, and then her heart froze. She could feel the blood resuming its pumping force within her.

Amy had folded her palms exactly how she had done when she was in the room earlier in the morning. Was that a coincidence? Mrs. Winters knew her daughter very well, she knew the body language of her daughter, too. Not in her lifetime had she folded her palms, one on top of the other, and rested them neatly on her lap while sitting in a straight posture.

It was then that Mrs. Winters noticed how neatly her hair was combed and braided and styled. It was not an act of carelessness, as she had perceived previously; it was a unique style that suited Amy. A style she had never adopted before.

What's wrong with you, Stella? Teenagers change all the time, and just because her palms are placed that way doesn't mean she is a monster.

Mrs. Winters shrugged the thought of all that had happened; it was a dream. Had she not woken up in her bed after passing out in Amy's room? Amy wouldn't have been able to lift her mother and tuck her into her bed without bringing her back to consciousness. And the room was spotlessly clean, too. Mrs. Winters was mentally assessing the situation when she thought of having a nap to clear her head.

A nap did her wonders; it solved most of the problems in her life. She was amazed to see her bed had been perfectly made.

Poor Amy, she thought, how thoughtful of her to make my bed when I have been having horrible thoughts about her. Mrs. Winters felt immensely guilty for her nightmare; she was absolutely certain that it was indeed a nightmare and nothing else. But then, she reached for the holy water she had placed on her side table in a glass. She was planning to sprinkle it on Amy and in her room.

The glass of water was gone.

There was no trace of any glass of water ever being there.

CHAPTER 3

WHO ARE YOU

ALL?

Mrs. Winters sat frozen on her bed, staring at her side table where the glass of holy water should have still been there. She felt a cold pack of ice had engulfed her entire body in a freezing and chilly manner, one that suffocated her. She tried to open her mouth, call her daughter, and ask her if she had removed the glass and why she had done that. Why had she even been in the room? For Mrs. Winters, her room was a holy place where people like Amy were not very welcome.

She was pondering over the thoughts that ran through her mind when her door knocked.

That dream…

"Excuse me, but I was wondering if you wanted to have breakfast?" Amy was standing at the door with her palms folded near her crotch area. It was very odd. The loose strand of hair that was previously bothering Amy was now tucked and secured in a neat bun. And was she wearing ironed clothes?

Jesus Christ…

Under any other circumstances, Mrs. Winters would have danced in joy to have such a massive transformation of her daughter. It was indeed a moment of joy to see the occasional disorganized Amy become a presentable and highly likable person, and the usual malfunctioning of her wardrobe was now switched, which was slightly alarming for Mrs. Winters. She took in Amy's choice of dress and her accent, and her mind raced back to the dream.

"Eggs, toast, or pancakes?" Amy asked her again. Her posture had not budged. It did not seem like Amy at all.

Flash. The sight of Amy folding her palms exactly that way in her bed. Flash. Amy's mouth was covered in blood. Flash. Amy's growling and walking sideways. Flash. Amy was talking in a Scottish accent. Flash. Amy tilted her head and asked Mrs. Winters to throw away the water. Flash. Amy addressed her mother using her first name.

It was as though Mrs. Winters was in a studio, modeling for the most gruesome nightmare ever for a contest. Surely, if there had been such a thing as to reward anyone with the most disturbing nightmare, Mrs. Winters would have had a trophy by now.

How could that be a coincidence? The demeanor that Amy had now adopted was exactly like….what the demon had named her? Patricia? Mrs. Winters vividly recalled how Amy had asked an invisible creature named 'Patricia,' and that had made or turned Amy into Patricia.

"Are you not hungry, eh?" Amy asked with an impatient scoff.

"Amy?" Mrs. Winters gasped. Almost whispered.

"We don't have time for this," Amy said dismissively and left the room. "Breakfast will be ready in 10." She spoke as she walked towards the kitchen.

We? Did Amy say 'we?'

Mrs. Winters shook her head. It was still spinning from all that had unfolded since morning.

Stella she is a grown woman. She can assume some responsibility, can't she? And why would that be a bad thing if she is asking for breakfast? Grow up, Stella. She probably took the glass and drank it after cleaning the house.

Mrs. Winters lay in her bed again and closed her eyes. She could hear Amy distantly humming in the background. The outside world was sane. The cars were honking, children were rushing to school, and adults were driving to their workplaces; it was all intact, the usual normalcy of everyday life. Amidst all that, there was her daughter, Amy. Now, just a few days back, everything had been normal. Well, normal had a different definition with Mrs. Winters. The normal life of hers and her daughter was about waking up in the morning, getting ready for the day, taking the trash out, and cleaning the house. Amy would start to paint in her room, mostly, and at times, she would take her paintings to somewhere only she knew. There were times when Amy would hang out with her friends or read a book that, too, was in her room.

But there was never a day when Mrs. Winters had woken up to find Amy covered in blood with a dead cat and possibly a dead body in her room, changing voices and shifting to a decent woman with a Scottish accent while being a gruesome devil.

Am I going insane? Mrs. Winters couldn't help but think. She reached for her Bible on the bookshelf she had in her room. It was gone. She frantically searched for it, but it was no use. The holy book was gone, as if it had formed legs and ran away from her room, just like the glass of holy water.

Maybe I left it in Amy's room? I was reading it last night, and with all the…the dead cat…No. Stella, it was a dream. Amy sitting up in bed as though an invisible force was lifting her. Was that a dream, too?

Mrs. Winters put those thoughts aside and focused on her normal routine. At this time, she was to take the trash out and make another cup of coffee. She took a deep breath and left her room. Amy was busy making something very aromatic. Mrs. Winters could feel her stomach begging her for food. The aroma had hit her nostrils and reached straight to her heart. The vanilla scent with honey was what she used to have during her early days. Mrs. Winters felt nostalgia drowning her, thankfully subduing the pathetic thoughts she was constantly having, much against her will.

She picked up the trash from under the sink, wrapped it, and left her house. It was unusually heavy that day. God, what had I put in it? She thought as she opened the lid. The recycled items were to be disposed of in a separate lid, while the organic waste had to be thrown separately. Mrs. Winters lifted the organic bag with effort, which made her sweat. She casually glanced at her kitchen window; Amy was whisking something in a bowl. She then thought that eggshells and orange peels could hardly account for all that weight. What was inside it? She couldn't help but open the top of the bag and take a peek. There was a dead cat and lots of clogged, thick black hair. She couldn't get her eyes away, so she stared at the ghastly items. The hair was actually blond, but something dark had turned it black. There were traces of maroon and brown on some of the strands of the hair. It was shaped in a perfect round, as though there was a head underneath the congealed locks.

Mrs. Winters shot a look towards her kitchen. Amy was standing by the window, her palms on the glass, with a wide grin. The same grin that was on her face when she had that nightmare. The same grinning face, or the creature, had asked for Patricia, and Amy had sat up in her bed like a spider crawling backwards.

Amy's grin did not subside. She continued to smile wider and wider at her mother. Mrs. Winters knew she would have to go in the house and save her daughter. As she walked inside, Amy's gaze followed her with that dreadful grin.

Mrs. Winters wanted some clarity, some answers, and a definite closure. Who was that creature walking around in her daughter's body? And what was that hairy ball? A head? God, no, please. Anything but that.

Mrs. Winters entered her home and went to the kitchen with heavy steps.

"Are you Amy?" The question had come out bluntly and with an air of annoyance that dominated the nature of curiosity in the question.

Amy's head turned around slyly. Thankfully, she was not grinning and seemed somewhat different than how she had looked when she was at the window. Her gaze was protruding, and she had the same expression that Mrs. Winters had seen on dead animals. That dead cat was as dead as the eyes of her daughter, who was very much alive and making breakfast for her.

"Why do you ask, Stella?" Amy smiled, "Did I not care for you well enough?"

"Stella?" Mrs. Winters felt her ribcage shaking. Her knees felt weak.

"We know your name. We know you. And your daughter, too, Stella. You need not worry. She is safe with us." Amy spoke. She gestured her palm as though there was an annoying bee around her.

"What is all this…" Mrs. Winters couldn't speak. Her mouth was wide open with disbelief and horror.

"You don't know?" Amy scoffed and returned to the kitchen counter, whisking the batter for the pancakes.

"Are …you... Patricia?" Mrs. Winters choked on her words. Her voice seemed to come from afar, a distant land that had no life. Only a barren land with nothing but death around it.

"Why, yes, there you are, not so idiot as some of us think," Amy flipped the omelet on the stove and spoke without looking behind her to see her pale white mother, looking like a ghost.

"Amy….the devil has…possessed you….my baby…" Mrs. Winters felt she would break down in tears and wail and sob, but her body had frozen itself. She was not even reacting to a new character in her daughter's body.

Patricia.

"I am Patricia Waters. We met earlier this morning, Stella. I offered to clean the mess, remember?"

So it wasn't a nightmare. It was real. And ugly. Patricia Waters was now Amy Winters.

Jesus Christ…

"Wha…wh….what…is   th…that   thing…in….in…in the….bag…hair…human….blood…" Mrs. Winters could not speak. She felt her body had stopped functioning, and at any moment, the angel of death would come and rescue her. She actually hoped to die. It was her only escape from what she had to encounter.

"It was, uh, how do I put it, let's say, Stella, oh, God, look at you," Amy put her hands to her mouth and rushed for a glass of water.

"Have this, my, my, you don't look well at all." Amy's peppermint breath touched Mrs. Winters' face. She would have sold her soul for this new, hygiene-conscious Amy under any other circumstances. But the situation was a lot different than anything normal.

The pounding in her head ceased momentarily. She gulped down water and asked for more, not caring whether it was that scanty devil, the graceful Patricia, or Abraham Lincoln. The world could fuck itself for all she cared. She was dehydrated; that explained why she had passed out in the room earlier. Water, the heavenly liquid, was all she wanted. The last time she had had anything to drink besides coffee seemed like a distant memory.

"You poor thing," Amy brushed her mother's hair from her forehead and gently kissed it.

Mrs. Winters flinched but didn't resist. She felt too weak.

"Food is right here. Give me a minute," Amy said and rushed to the kitchen. She brought an omelet and pancakes for Mrs. Winters.

"Finish it, you poor darling; you don't want to annoy him again, do you?" Amy gently patted Mrs. Winters' shoulders and let her have the meal in silence.

The dreadful questions hung in the air. Who was Patricia Waters, and who the fuck was him? Him, who? Amy had said the same thing, 'You are disturbing him.' And now, Patricia had warned of annoying that same entity.

CHAPTER 4

GO HOME, STELLA

Mrs. Winters didn't have much to do that day; most of the chores were taken care of by Amy or the entity in Amy. Lunch was prepared, and the house was clean with a lovely citrus scent. It seemed as though Mrs. Winters had been teleported to another dimension where things could never go ugly or nasty, where she had a lovely obedient daughter who responsibly not just cleaned her room but also the entire house, made heavenly lunches pancakes, and took regular showers herself. It seemed too eerie to be a part of the world where Amy had distanced herself and not spoken to her mother in her entire life, except for when it was absolutely necessary. Amy had confined herself in her room and not given a rat's ass whether the house reeked of dead bodies or citrusy scents; she had barely bothered to ask her mother for tea, let alone cook lunch or breakfast for her.

There had to be something wrong with her, Mrs. Winters thought. She had seen enough in her life to understand that whatever was happening with her daughter was not natural.

Father Samuel...he'll have the answers.

Mrs. Winters thought to herself and decided to leave for the church. It was time for the holy and the wise to intervene and put things straight. If there was anyone who could tell exactly what was wrong with her daughter, it was Father Samuel, or so she believed. Father Samuel was a psychiatrist and rarely practiced exorcism on anyone. He mostly attributed the symptoms to a mental disorder, but he was sure to help those in need of an actual exorcism. Mrs. Winters was more than certain that her daughter was possessed, and there was nothing psychological but diabolical going on with Amy.

Mrs. Winters took her coat and left the house.

"Lunch, Stella? Be home on time; you'd love to eat with us," Amy had called out from the kitchen as Mrs. Winters was leaving. She flinched and didn't respond. Us?

She picked pace and walked towards the church; the craziness was too much for her to deal with. She could hear the same horrid tune that Amy was humming in the background.

The weather was dauntingly pleasant that day; the clouds and the breeze had coincided to reveal just enough sunlight for warmth while concealing it for excessive heat. Mrs. Winters, on any other day, would have marveled at the beauty and the tender effect the weather was having on her. Just like she would have wholeheartedly appreciated Amy talking to her, being chatty, and making lunches for her. But the situation at hand was far too dramatic.

Mrs. Winters walked to the church and greeted Father Samuel. He was standing outside, adjusting something in his car.

"Father," Mrs. Winters said. It was hard for her not to burst into tears.

"Mrs. Winters," he said. He managed to get out of his car and brush his clothes. He was a tall man with a wide forehead. His deep-set eyes and a square jawline made him look like a square figurine from the toy shop.

"I am.... not well…father…" she began to weep.

"Mrs. Winters, come here," he took her to the pavement, away from the church. "What happened?" he was concerned.

"Amy…" Mrs. Winters couldn't speak. How could she when she had been through so much…the only thin fabric of sanity she had in her life was her daughter, and now she was being taken away from her. How could she not lose it all and burst out?

"She is…" Mrs. Winters choked on her words and coughed.

"Hold it, please come and sit down," Father Samuel led her into the car and made her sit down on the front seat. He gave her water in a cup that he kept in his car.

"Please, calm down and tell me," he assured her.

There was a cross dangling on the rearview mirror and an idol of Jesus and Mary stuck on the space above the dashboard. Mrs. Winters looked at the cross and wept some more.

"Okay, take your time," he gave her some tissues and waited patiently.

Despite the pleasant weather, Mrs. Winters had begun to sweat.

"I am better now," she panted lightly.

"Actually, not better, but at least I am not as troubled…as I am in the house…" Mrs. Winters whimpered.

"What is going on, Mrs. Winters? I'd really like to know. You can come by my office if you like." Father Samuel proposed.

"No, I don't think I can wait, not that long, I mean…him…" Mrs. Winters stammered. She was not making any sense at all.

"Who is he? Is there some guy bothering your daughter?" Father Samuel said. "I can call the police." He picked up his phone, but Mrs. Winters grabbed his hands.

"NO," she almost shrieked. There was a possible decapitated head in her trash, which would require a lot of explaining. And how on earth could she explain that it was not her daughter without sounding sane? Wasn't Father Samuel also someone who didn't believe in the paranormal, not as much as a father should anyway? Was he the right person to talk about this?

"Mrs. Winters, you need to tell me what is going on," he said. He squinted his eyes and looked at Mrs. Winters, wondering if the woman needed help herself and not the daughter.

"We can go to the office. I was on my way there already," Father Samuel suggested.

"All right," Mrs. Winters said. It would give her more time to think about how she could possibly avoid that human head and still ask for Father's help. She didn't want her daughter to commit murders, but she also didn't want her to rot in jail for a crime she didn't commit.

But that body belongs to Amy, and the possession and the entity; those are for Father Samuel to figure out.

The drive to Father Samuel's clinic was in complete silence. He was busy making mental notes about Mrs. Winters' reaction and what she was probably worried about; he used all of his mental faculties to think of all the possible outcomes or reasons that could upset her to this extent. Was it an accident where her daughter had been hurt by a man? Or was someone from the school molesting her? Or was it something demonic? Since it was him whom Mrs. Winters had relied on, it has to be something sinister…and that he could be a ghost, a demon, or the devil himself?

"Can I have some more water, please?" Mrs. Winter said.

"Yeah, sure, the bottle is in the dashboard. You can reuse the cup." He said while driving.

"How long do we reach your office?" Mrs. Winters asked him. She was getting tired and feeling drained, as though every ounce of her energy had already been consumed.

"Just five more minutes approximately." Father Samuel responded.

"All right," Mrs. Winters said dryly.

The rest of the journey was in silence. None spoke a word. Mrs. Winters drank from the cup and placed it back to where it was. Once they arrived, she unbuckled her seatbelt.

"Do you mind waiting for me for just a while? I will be back in no time. I have something to take care of, and…" Father Samuel was apologetic. He wore an expression that told her that it was the least favorable thing he was doing, but it had to be done. That there was indeed something that only he could handle. A psycho patient?

Cut it out, Stella, let him be.

She smiled weakly and said, "Sure, Father, take your time."

"All right, I will be back to take you to the office. Do you want some music till then?" he suggested.

"No, thanks. I'd just like some peace and quiet." Mrs. Winters said, rubbing the back of her neck.

"Sure. I'll put the kettle for some coffee," he smiled and left. The car door shut with a gentle bang.

Mrs. Winters tapped on her fingers and counted to ten. She closed her eyes and took deep breaths. Each one lasts longer than the usual breathing pattern.

"Stella…." A voice whispered in her ear.

She opened her eyes and bolted upright. Her head spun 180 degrees to see if there was anyone behind her, but there was nobody.

"Stellaaaa…. go home…." The same voice whispered in her other ear. A voice she knew too well. She had just heard that voice recently.

Mrs. Winters didn't turn her head. Instead, she froze on the spot.

It was his voice.

CHAPTER 5

YOUR WISH IS MY

COMMAND

Stella Winters was unable to move in the car. She stopped breathing and didn't dare to look on her left side. She thought of Ephesians 6:11 and wanted to recite the verse, but then, a voice broke the silence.

"He is not here to protect you. Your God died on the cross, didn't he," the voice then broke into a shrilling laughter. A menacing, evil laughter.

Mrs. Winters couldn't move, and this time, her body had a layer of ice wrapped around it. She breathed with great difficulty as her head motioned upwards; an invisible force was groping for her neck, choking her and seizing any signs of life she had had in her.

"Jes…us…hel…pp…" she couldn't speak.

She croaked and gasped.

Her ear was buzzing with sounds that didn't make sense. Some of them were random chants that she had heard somewhere but where she couldn't quite figure out. Some were the rhythmic hymns in a deep male voice. Then, there was a voice among the others. It was a very high-pitched, shrilling, and piercing voice, except it was a cackling laughter and not a voice, but more of a sound in the background.

Who are you all?

"Mrs. Winters?" Samuel opened the door of the car and bent down. She had turned white.

"Oh, dear God, did I put the glass up? I am terribly sorry, I shouldn't have let you wait here," Samuel fumbled with the buttons on his door. He was genuinely ashamed of the trouble he had caused Mrs. Winters, but looking at her, it seemed more than just a minor inconvenience; it looked as though she had returned from the dead. As though she were, in fact, more dead than alive.

"Mrs. Winters?" Father Samuel asked her again. He had turned down the glasses of the car doors and opened his door wide to let air in. He held a cup of glass in his hand to offer her, but she did not respond. She just stared at him, point blank, with no response at all.

"Mrs. Winters, are you alright? You don't look…okay…are you?" He asked her.

She was quiet. Her eyes darted on Samuel's face with bewilderment.

"He is here," she whispered in an almost inaudible volume.

"I am sorry, what?" Father Samuel looked confused.

"He is here." Mrs. Winters said.

"Alright, we will discuss this once we are inside." Father Samuel said and helped Mrs. Winters step out of his car and enter his clinic. He knew he would have to record any information from Stella Winters and keep it in his files. He could not have a session outside the clinic. It was against the rules he had set for himself.

"Right, so Mrs. Winters, you can lie down," Father Samuel helped her adjust on the couch. She stared at the ceiling for some time, then restored her gaze at Father Samuel.

"Forgive me, Father, for I have sinned." She began.

"Stella, this is not…what have you done this time?" He corrected himself and watched her.

Over the years, he had seen and treated many patients. Most of whom were schizophrenic, paranoid, depressed, and psychotic.

"Have you been taking your medicines?" he asked her.

"No," she replied meekly. She looked down at her hands and bit a nail nervously.

"So, what is bothering you?" He asked her. He had a pen and a notepad in front of him. It was usually not a very welcoming sight for Mrs. Winters; she preferred him as someone next to her, someone she could talk to or share her problems with. The role of a psychiatrist behind a desk didn't suit her – it agitated her. So he had avoided doing that, but that day, he had sat behind the desk on purpose, to see if Stella would mind. She didn't.

Samuel Brown was a renowned psychiatrist in his mid-40s. His expertise in working on patients and treating them was well crafted over the years he had served in the field of mental science. The brain is a network of complications; he had put it during his casual hangouts with his friends at the club. A modest drinker, bachelor, and serious professional, Samuel Brown knew crazy when he saw one.

One night at the bar, he had an argument with one of his friends, Jerry. He believed that a doctor should not call his patients crazy and, instead, should use euphemisms like mentally challenged, disabled, or something else, but never the word crazy. Samuel had voiced his opinion about calling a spade a spade. And that there was absolutely nothing wrong with saying a person was crazy when he was having episodes of schizophrenia, paranoia, or even split personality.

"But that is a disorder, ain't it?" Jerry had argued while gulping his beer.

"Yeah, and that's what makes them crazy. Abnormal." Samuel added.

"But why crazy? Why can't they just be different with their heads?" Jerry said.

"Listen, what do you call a person with influenza? What do you call a person with hepatitis? A sick person, right? Or someone with a different functioning immune system? For fuck sake, a person not acting normally is bound to be crazy." Samuel had said in a calm and cool voice.

"That's rude." Jerry held his ground.

"And truth, too. I am not one of those idiots who sugarcoat things and say, oh, you're fat shaming, or body shaming, or this and that. A fat person is fat. Get the fuck over it, will you?" Samuel said.

"I give up, but crazy is a harsh word," Jerry said.

"And a word we doctors use more often than you think." Samuel had concluded his argument.

He flipped his pen on the desk and waited patiently.

"Mrs. Winters," he asked her politely.

She was silent.

"You mentioned something about your daughter," he said.

"Who?" Mrs. Winters looked up with a disgusted look on her face. Her features had contorted to form a frown that somehow seemed it didn't belong on that face.

"Amy. You mentioned there was something about her…can we talk about that?" Samuel spoke in a calm tone.

"She is dead." Mrs. Winters said.

"How did she die?"

"I killed her."

"Mrs. Winters, have you been getting enough sleep?" He asked her.

"I don't need to sleep." Mrs. Winters had a guttural voice as though she was a dummy doll, and a ventriloquist was behind her pulling the strings.

"I don't sleep. Ich schlafe überhaupt nicht."

"Are you Mrs. Winters?" Samuel slowly walked towards Mrs. Winters, his eyes not breaking contact with her for even a split second. He sat on the chair and faced the armchair where Mrs. Winters was sitting with her face resting on her knees. She had embraced them and was patting them. An act of self-soothing, Samuel observed but didn't say anything.

Groaning. No response, but just groaning.

"Hello. My name is Samuel. I am your Doctor."

"I don't care."

"I see. Mrs. Winters, you need to sleep, eat, and take your medications on time." He tried to get closer to her, but she flinched. So, he maintained his distance and looked at her. The wonders of the human mind had amazed him — how a man could shift into a different personality yet have the same medium was still a field of science he knew so little about. His diagnosis was to temporarily put the patient to sleep and then hypnotize them to get their inner fears out. Once that was established, he would sedate his patients and hypnotize them again to forget those fears. The patients would then go on to live their lives along with the medications that balanced their hormones and the chemical wiring of the brain.

"What is that?" Mrs. Winters pointed to the rosemary placed on the table.

"Oh, that is what we call rosemary. Do you want to see it?"

Mrs. Winters glared at him.

"You all are idiots," she cackled.

"Are you Mrs. Winters?" He asked her.

"No," she hissed and seethed. She twisted her head in the air and put her knees up to sit like a spider. "Das bin ich nicht." She hissed again.

Interesting, Samuel thought to himself. He had invested most of his spare time in studying human behaviour and its development; he was well aware that the human mind was capable of doing things beyond what most of us comprehend and label as normal. This was a primary example.

"Who am I speaking with?" he asked her.

"*Halt den Mund*," she spoke in a whisper.

"I speak German, too, but I'd like to know who I am talking to. Telling me to shut up will not help the conversation, right?" He asked her with a polite smile.

"Ba…Ba…Ba…" she breathed.

"Yes, go on." He encouraged her.

"Baal." She raised her voice and glared at him.

"I see, Baal. Hello, I am Dr. Samuel. Nice to meet you. What are you doing here in my clinic?" His tone was warm and friendly.

No response.

"Where is Stella?"

"With us."

"Can I talk to her?"

Laughter. Multiple voices were simultaneously laughing.

"*Ich…. ICH….ICH BEN….*" Mrs. Winters spoke some gibberish in German with her hands raised.

"I don't quite understand; you are what?"

Silence. Her hands dropped down on her thighs, and she stared at a spot on the floor.

Interesting. Very interesting.

Samuel reached for the injection he had for patients when they desperately needed one. He often had to use it with Mrs. Winters, and this time was no exception. But just before he could subdue her with the injection, he saw her peacefully asleep on the couch, as though the entire episode with Baal had just been an imagination.

He reached for the recorder he had installed in his office. It was used to record sessions, and at the end, Dr. Samuel would add his notes and his conclusive remarks.

"Patient is showing signs of severe personality disassociation. High chance of some past trauma lingering in the mind. Need to book a session for hypnosis. Prescription includes increased dosage of Maddoxil to 500 mg. Concern rate: Moderate." He placed the recorder on his table and turned around.

"Mrs. Winters, I thi…" he broke off mid-sentence.

There was no one in the room.

CHAPTER 6

WOULD YOU KILL

FOR ME?

Dr. Samuel had prepared for the day. He had to examine five of his patients and then head back home for a hearty dinner of pork belly and ribs. He stretched his arms and yawned. Resting on his table was the recorder with the file of Mrs. Winters uploaded.

His secretary buzzed in.

"I am so sorry, Doctor. I was stuck in the traffic. I, uh, I am sorry. I will get your files in no time." She explained apologetically.

"It is absolutely fine, I managed. In fact, I tended to a patient just a while ago. She left, though. Did you see Mrs. Winters going out of our clinic?" he asked her.

"No, I did not. She may have left before I came in." the secretary said. She was out of breath.

"Calm down, sit here, have some water. And you can refill the jug when you're on your way out." He gave her a glass of water, which she gulped right away.

"Are you wearing that perfume? The one Stevenson gave you?" he chuckled.

"Yes, it is. I love Gucci Guilty. It's really great. I haven't seen him in a while, though."

"He'll come around, and Heather, you look great today," Samuel said with a smile.

"Oh, look at you," she blushed. Underneath the layers of makeup, Samuel could see a little girl blushing. Heather Wilson was a blonde, tall, and lean woman with a proportionate figure for her age. Her mid-30s had not given her the blues, and she liked to spend her time in the company of people much younger than her age. Her love life was never organized, nor was it a structured pattern of successful relationships. It was like a horror movie or a zombie chase; anything could happen at any time. She sometimes wondered if she liked the unpredictability in her relationships. The air of not knowing what would come next or who would come next, but that uncertainty came with tides of pain and waves of depression; both were what put off Heather for the next venture. Every time she had her heart broken, she would vow never to get involved again, but then, with a cute smile here and a compliment there, she would ride the same boat without any life jacket, too.

"What are you thinking?" Samuel asked her.

"Oh, nothing. I just have the daily tasks to look into. Nothing much."

"Lie."

"What? No, come on, I am not…." She scoffed and chuckled.

"Yes. What is it?"

"Nothing, really…I mean…"

"Yes, what is it? Tell me." He pushed her.

"I just think why do I end up falling in love over and over, and whether this is a psychological condition…I mean, look at Stevens; he is all nice and charming, but then I caught him staring at other girls at the pub. And I am sure he is doing more than just checking them out when he is with them. So, I was just thinking if I am following a pattern." She let it out.

"Yes, you do. And this is poor judgment and decision-making, nothing psychological." He said in his usual calm voice.

"What do you mean? I don't get it." She looked confused. Absentmindedly, she combed her hair with her fingers.

"I mean, you jump into this feeling you call love without thinking about what the other person is like. Whether he is worth investing time and energy, or whether he is just there to have some fun and move on." He said.

"Oh, you mean I need to do Sherlock Holmes work before falling in love?" she seemed slightly offended.

"No, I am just saying, why do you need someone to validate you? You can be who you are, your true lovable self, with no jerks as lovers." He sighed.

"Ah, right." She replied. "I should get to my desk."

"Relax, we don't have the first patient until an hour." He said.

"Sorry, you had to go through the schedule yourself. It's just the traffic that was so annoying." She said.

"Heather, it's fine. Tell me, do you know anything about ghosts? Or demons?" he asked her in a casual manner.

"Yes, I mean, not much, but yes, I have heard a thing or two. Why? What happened?" she was curious to know. Samuel was never a man believing in ghosts or the paranormal; he always had his stance of anyone or anything unseen as nonexistent, which meant the spirit world was all bullshit for him. He believed in science and had to portray the image of a religious man. He was not even remotely religious. In fact, he was the one refuting Trinity and Jesus dying on the cross. Most of his Christian friends had joined the debate but with no use. His arguments and years and years of self-study had made him realize that there may be a God, but He definitely didn't send His son to save the world. That logic didn't fit with him.

"What happened?" she asked him again.

"No, I mean, I was wondering if someone could have some funny ideas while watching a movie. A horror movie? And adopt that person and pretend to be that entity?" he said.

"Samuel? You need to be a bit more open with me." She raised an eyebrow.

"Nothing…maybe…I am the one running my imagination wild," he laughed.

"A second opinion doesn't hurt," she added softly.

"Here is what we can do. I had a really awkward session with Mrs. Winters today. And I am wondering if she is influenced by anything sinister. Now, I know how you like dark arts, magic, and the occult; I know you are a big fan. So we can discuss somethings about it over coffee?" Samuel pursed her lips after he finished talking.

"Yes, sure. I have some doughnuts. Do you want any?" she asked.

"No. I don't eat sugary treats, and you know it." He smiled.

"I don't mind a boost of sugar myself. I mean, this topic sounds interesting, and I would love to delve deep into it. I'll get coffee in a minute." Heather left the room and reached for the kitchen behind her desk. She put the coffee in the machine and waited, listening to the very familiar buzzing of the machine. She had often thought of the machine as a mother, producing the elixir of life from its body and letting her live for yet another day.

There was a strong stench of something rotting that hit her nose.

"Oh, fuck," she gasped for air. She searched frantically for the source of the smell but couldn't find anything.

"Probably a dead rat in the vent," she spoke slowly.

She got the mugs ready, placed her doughnut on a plate, and reached the room. She tried her best to ignore the smell and opened the windows wide so that it would be less embarrassing when the patients started flooding in.

"There is a dead rat somewhere in the kitchen." She said as she placed the mug in front of Dr. Samuel on his table.

"There is?" he looked surprised.

"Yes, it is stinking there," she replied.

"So, you wanted to know dark arts. Since when are you into this voodoo business?" she laughed and sipped on her coffee.

"No, I am not. I am just curious if a devout catholic could be interested in dark arts." He added.

"So, what in particular do you want to know? What can you do with magic, or what else?" She took a bite from her doughnut and said with a mouthful.

"Yes, let's start with how does it all begin?"

"Okay, so let's say you have a wish. It could be anything like getting your lover or getting loads of money, or whatever, healing or even cursing someone. You make a pact with the devil." Heather said solemnly.

"The devil?" Dr. Samuel laughed and cast a glance at his degree framed on the wall.

"All those years I spent studying so hard about the human mind, and here we are discussing a component of the human mind. The devil is nothing but a.."

"But a real entity, Doctor. Your science has not disproved it, so don't give me that," she replied.

"So, you were saying," he gestured for her to continue.

"Yes, so you make a deal with the devil." She said with another bite of the doughnut.

"What does….how does it work?" he asked

"Your wish will be granted. Even if it's impossible." Heather said.

"Okay, so what do you mean impossible? I mean, how much can you get from the dark arts and black magic?" Samuel had leaned in to focus on Heather and her revelations.

"You can bring the dead to life. You can get someone to love you; you can also get someone to hate someone, cause divorces, do whatever," she replied.

"Whatever? Even…kill someone?" Samuel was hesitant.

"Yes, or bring the dead back to life, like I said. You have to pay homage to the devil, agree to his terms, and then your wish is granted. There is an entire section of tantra teachings in Hinduism, which is very similar to what the ancient civilizations have been doing, invoking devils and their companions. The Abrahamic religions condemn it, and the Koran of Muslims says not to take the devil as a friend. He is an open enemy to Adam's children. But we have forgotten what the God of the Bible, Torah, and Koran has taught us. That tantra I was talking about includes sitting in a dark corner, not bathing, not eating or drinking anything except for your own excrement for a week. During this time, a demon will appear, and you have to have sex with him/her. It's mostly a goddess, Kali goddess, in her vicious form. Once it's over, she will make a demand, and you will make a demand. And it's done." Heather had looked straight at Samuel while enlightening him with her knowledge about dark arts.

"Wow, okay, so…who are these devils?" he was interested now.

"Mostly, we can invoke Kali. She is used for destruction. Or other Hindu mythological gods…"

"Wait, you said mythological? So, they are not real gods?" Samuel asked her.

"Oh, for fuck sake, Doctor, what has gotten into you? Do you really believe that Odin was a god? And that he and his brothers killed Ymir, so did the world come into being? Or that Gaia had impregnated all living beings and gave birth to gods, or that Ra, Brahma, or Jesus are the creators? They didn't create themselves. This is what I am telling you. It has always been about worshipping the devil. These are demons, devils, Satan, and his followers, renaming and reshaping themselves to harm human beings. None of them are true creators." Heather replied earnestly.

"I see, so can you name any actual demons, the ones who haven't renamed themselves or…"

"You are spooking me, Doctor. What are you into now? Witchcraft? Voodoo dolls? Black magic or the tantric magic?" Heather laughed and helped herself with another donut.

"No, I am just curious." Samuel lied.

"Okay, so, what do you want to know again? Sorry, your keen interest had me off. I can't help but think one of these days, I might encounter a dead cat or something in your cabin."

"A dead cat?" Samuel asked with a frown.

"Yes, a dead cat. It is used as animal sacrifice when you are worshipping the devil. Animal or human sacrifice. It is mandatory to please the devil."

"Can I have those names? Any demons that are really actual demons and known for being evil and all?" Samuel insisted.

"Yeah, sure. So we can start with, um, what's the name, uh, yeah, Baphomet. We have that Lucifer. And we also have that Beelzebub. And then Baal…and th…"

"Wait, what?" Samuel could feel his heart beating faster.

"What? You asked for the nam…"

"What did you say just now?" He interrupted her.

"I said the names."

"Yeah, can you repeat those?"

"Okay, so there is Beelzebub, there is Baphomet, there is Baal…"

"Baal?" Samuel asked her. He could feel the hair rising on the back of his neck.

"Yes, Baal."

"Is he…a …"

"A demon. Yes, Baal is one of the chief demons." Heather said nonchalantly.

The door of the room flung open gently; the cleaning elderly lady was standing with a displeased expression.

"Did you guys lose your mind?" she scolded both the Doctor and his secretary. It was as though they were little kids being caught in an act or after a very dirty act.

"I don't understand, what?" Heather looked confused.

Dr. Samuel let Mrs. Stone speak to them that way; considering how old she was and how she needed a job, he let her be the way she was. Warm at heart but icy and acidic from the tongue.

"You left a dead cat for me to clean in the kitchen? God, these days, people have no manners and no respect for the elderly.

There is blood all over the place. Now, I have to mop the floor and scrub it…"

The voice trailed off as Mrs. Stone left, blabbering all sorts of injustice being done to her.

CHAPTER 7

THEY HAVE COME TO VISIT

US

The dark afternoon was like a sad goodbye to all that the day had to offer; the chirping birds, the lively streets, and the bustling of the walkways – none of that mattered to, or compared to what was going on inside the Winters' residence. The walls had grown like shackles of a prisoner, and the interior was unusually dark and gloomy, despite all the cleaning Amy had done in the morning, the evening painted an entirely different picture of the house. It looked haunted, screaming and begging for some normalcy, for some sign of life, or at the very least, it looked as though there was a touch of madness attached to the aura of the house.

Mrs. Winters had reached her home, at what time, she couldn't remember, but she had rested on a sofa ever since she was back. Her head was pounding, and she wanted to shower. There was a strange reeking, an unknown smell of rust, and excrement on her clothes. She couldn't figure out what had happened, and when had she passed out, and when had she sat on the sofa.

Stella Winters was a regular patient of Doctor Samuel. She had made regular visits to him, and he had seemed to heal her. Her mental state had drastically improved over the years.

She closed her eyes and it was an imagery of the least pleasant things in her life.

Flash. An altar. Flash. A decapitated head. Flash. Him…. Flash…the black shadowy figure…Flash. A dead cat… Flash. Amy…

"Amy…." Mrs. Winters woke up from her sleep, and yelled. It was a cry intended to recall a person, and not so much as to call a person.

"Aym…my dear Aym…" Mrs. Winters said aloud.

"Mother?" A voice broke her trance.

It was Amy.

"What? Who? Oh, yes, oh, God…are you okay?" Mrs. Winters stumbled on her words, and tried to form a sensible sentence for a rational mind.

"Yes, you called my name…I mean the other one…Aym…you didn't…I mean you stopped using that name a long time ago. What happened?" She said.

"I don't know, I went to the church, and then I, I guess I didn't go anywhere because I must have been dreaming it."

Was it all a dream? Amy looks absolutely fine.

"Oh, you must have passed out. You look tired," she said with a poker face.

Is she hiding guilt? Is this her cover for killing cats in her room, and possibly a human, too…No, Stella, she is still your baby…

"Come here, darling," Mrs. Winters said. Her chin had begun to quiver, as her eyes started to water. Tears of relief, mixed with a longing sensation of having found someone who was previously lost. Mrs. Winters held on to Amy and sobbed.

"I love you my baby," she wept. It was more of a declaration. It seemed as though Mrs. Winters had faced a tiring battle, and was facing an entire army of the devils, ghosts, spirits, demons, jinns, and every ounce of evil put together.

"Lord…I love you my child…" she wailed again.

There was a shift in Amy's body.

Outside, a dog had started barking really loudly. Mrs. Winters could feel Amy stiffening and clenching her jaw. It was as though she had transcended to some other place, and someone else had overtaken her body.

There was a change in Amy's breathing. Her soft hair rubbed against Mrs. Winters' cheek, which was the most comforting touch in the world, Mrs. Winters could swear. But then, the gentle presence of her only child turned into a feeling of uneasiness.

Mrs. Winters could recall how during the times when Amy was an infant, she would snuggle Mrs. Winters and rest her little head on her mother's shoulders. The gentle touch of a life that had sprung from Mrs. Winters' womb was way too comforting to put into words. Mrs. Winters had spent hours and hours, just holding the baby in her arms and humming a gentle song to her. It relaxed Amy.

The times had changed. Amy Winters was no longer an infant, she had grown up to be a beautiful lady, much like her mother in her youth. Mrs. Winters ignored the shift in Amy's body. Usually, Amy was not fond of returning hugs, or being physically affectionate with her mother. She was keeping her distance ever since she had grown up.

But standing in the living room was not Amy. It didn't feel like Amy.

Mrs. Winters frowned slightly, noticing the shift. Her feelings subsided when Amy wrapped her arms around Mrs. Winters and chuckled lightly.

"Now, now, Stella, where have you been since morning. And why didn't you join us for lunch?" The Scottish accent sentence rang in Mrs. Winters' ears. She stood frozen, unable to move. She clenched her jaws and felt her knees giving away.

"We missed you, Stella," Amy spoke again.

"Did you miss us?" Amy giggled, and took a deep breath, "Well, we had baked chicken with mashed potatoes."

No response. Mrs. Winters could not move at all.

"What happened, Stella, I thought you liked us." Amy had started to laugh.

The voice was different. It came from the vocal cords of Amy, that part was true, but there was a slight alteration to how the sound produced had a quality of a foreign touch, as though someone was speaking in harmony with Amy.

Mrs. Winters breathes sharply, and let go of the grip she had on her daughter. Her arms released Amy, and she took a step back with her eyes down. She could feel Amy breathing hard, deep calculated breaths; was she meditating? Or planning something sinister?

"Oh, come on, don't be a daft," Amy gently patted Mrs. Winters' arm, which sent a shiver down her spine.

"Mom…Mama, mother, oh yes, mother…is that better?" Amy said again sarcastically with a smirk. The voice however, belonged to Patricia.

The expression on her face was different; squinted, sultry eyes with her jawline totally tension-free. Usually, Amy would clench her jaws when agitated, and Mrs. Winters would have to remind her to not do that. It had created a misalignment in her jaws, the left one was slightly delaying when Amy tried to open her mouth. This had resulted in Amy not being able to brush her teeth all the way back. And then, there was a series of dentist appointments, and regular scaling and cleaning, which further irritated Amy, and she clenched her jaws all the more. It was a loop of misery; Mrs. Winters had put it that way.

Mrs. Winters dared to look, she just had to. Even though every inch in her body told her to leave, to get the fuck out of the house, and never acknowledge the being her daughter had become; she chose to stand there frozen, finally making eye contact with Amy.

Fuck you, Stella…. run….

"Well…? What do you think? Do you like the lavender soap I used to shower? It was hectic, cleaning all the blood, you know," Amy scoffed, and gestured her palm. "I wanted something citrus, but then I settled with lavender. It's equally good, isn't it?"

"Amy?" Mrs. Winters was shivering.

"Oh, poor darling," Amy said. "You are sweating. My God Stella, you are about to pass out any minute, please sit down. I will bring you some water. Or how about lemonade? I have made some. Do you want to have a refreshing lemonade? We can chit chat after that, or if you want some peace, I can give you a foot massage to ease your worries." Amy chirped like a bird.

"I, uh, I…Amy…" Mrs. Winters could feel her senses leaving her, leaving her in this void with Patricia, or Amy, or him?

Amy needs help….

"No, we don't need your help, Stella." Patricia remarked from the kitchen.

"We don't need your help." He spoke.

"Mom, I don't need you." Amy spoke.

"We don't need you," a childish voice added the trio.

I am going crazy…are my thoughts not safe, too…. the church…I must….

"Stay home." Amy glared at her mother.

At that moment of time, it was hard to see whether it was Amy, or one of the others.

"Mom, the others have come to visit us." Amy said in her usual persona and demeanor, holding her mother's sweaty palm.

CHAPTER 8

WHY DID YOU BURY

ME?

The winds blew the useless dust particles at the walkway of the Winters' residence. The cars parked at the evening were giving an impression of a calm, and soothing time that people liked to spend with their families in the comfort of their homes. Almost all the neighbors of the Winters had a cozy evening, baked chicken pies, cakes, and chattering of people on the dining table. The kids had had their meals, and the parents were busy cleaning after dinner. Tables were swept clean with the last crumbs of the meal removed from the table. The plates were in the dishwashers, and the children brushed their teeth as a ritual before bed.

Overall, the town painted a lively picture, one that did not include any dead bodies, or killers in the house. The town had a very low rate of crimes, and people felt safe to leave their kids outside on the lawn, to play for hours, even after it got dark. Some mothers let the main doors open while their kids played, totally carefree and safe.

It felt to the residents that there was an unseen and an unknown safety net around the citizens – everyone was well-protected and secure inside it. The headlines of the newspaper contained good news which was a feast to the eyes of all those who sipped their morning coffee while scanning through it. The TV channels spoke of light-hearted comedy and drama, with not much wrong with that town. Locally, people greeted each other, and exchanged welcoming dinners and muffins with each other.

The house of Winters was an exception.

Mrs. Winters had not moved an inch. She felt blood, and all traces of life draining from her face, and down to her knees, which seemed pretty lifeless themselves. She knew if she dared to get up, run, or even crawl to the front door, her body would not cooperate, it would remain frozen and unmoved like a statue.

Flash. Baal's idol. Flash. Blood. Flash. Amy's hair. Flash. Voodoo doll. Flash. Amy's dead body.

The memories flooded in Mrs. Winters' head, and she cringed to keep them away.

"No," she screamed.

"I can't take it anymore," she shook her head.

"What happened, mother?" Amy asked her with a queer smile.

"Amy, you are alive, sweetheart…you are…"

The doorbell rang.

"You have a visitor," Amy said.

With all that had happened, it was hard for Mrs. Winters to clearly identify which of the others was it at that moment; was it Patricia? Amy? Him? And who was that little child who had spoken out loud whatever was going inside Mrs. Winters' head? Was it a ghost? A spirit.

"You don't want to keep him waiting, do you?" Amy said. She had prepared lemonade and adjusted two glasses on the table. "Go on, open the door, Stella."

"No, I want some answers from you." Mrs. Winters glared at Amy.

"Mom, that can wait." Amy said.

Wasn't there a pattern for shifting personalities? Or did it just happen so quickly? Amy and the others didn't need time to take turns now, they were abrupt, as though they were all sitting together with their attention on Mrs. Winters. That meant that he was there, too? Wasn't he? He was with the others? Of course he was, where else would he be? Wasn't he a creation of Amy's head? So if Amy had created Patricia, and the little child, that naturally means she had created him, too. He must be the devil. He wasn't created, but was probably the one why Amy was facing such things.

"What do you want to know from us?" Amy asked with a settled expression, indicating that it was a well-discussed topic and they had already come to a conclusion multiple times in the past. As far as Mrs. Winters could remember, this was the first time she was having that conversation with Amy.

"Get the door, Stella." Amy said nonchalantly; totally oblivious to the decapitated head and the dead cat in her room earlier that morning. Wasn't she afraid or worried about the police? Why didn't it ever hit her mind that Mrs. Winters may have called the cops, and asked someone to come and arrest her, and that she would now have to go to prison for the rest of her life? Why was she so okay… Normal…almost carefree…

"I need answers," Mrs. Winters said, staring at her daughter.

"Okay, let's do this then." Amy said.

"Who are you?" Mrs. Winters said.

"IHRE TOCHTER IST BEI UNS."

"My daughter is with you all?" Mrs. Winters repeated the claim made by Amy. The voice, this time, was the one that had a guttural effect to it.

It was him.

"Where is she? Where is Amy?"

"Oh, poor, poor darling," Amy smirked and said, "Do you not remember anything? You asked for this. You asked for all of this. You invited us. Things were just fine, but then, you forgot, Stella…do you still not remember?"

"REMEMBER WHAT?" Mrs. Winters shrieked in horror and disbelief. What was Amy talking about? Was she drunk, or high? Oh no, she neither of those. She was crazy as fuck. Amy had really lost her mind.

Flash. Blood. Flash. Amy's dead body. Flash. An idol. Flash.

"Did it help?" Amy smiled and asked her.

"How can you read my mind?" Mrs. Winters was panting. And sweating.

"The door, Mother, there is someone at the door." Amy said in her voice with pain in her eyes. And there was something else in her eyes, a hint of betrayal, or a streak of pain and panic at the same time. So she was worried that Mrs. Winters had called cops on her? Or was the pain associated with entirely something else? And had nothing to do with the visitor at the door?

There was only one way to find out.

And that was: to answer the fucking door.

CHAPTER 9

FORGIVE ME, FATHER, FOR I HAVE SINNED

With reluctant and shaky steps, Mrs. Winters reached the door. She paused and turned the knob.

It was Dr. Samuel at the door.

"Mrs. Winters," he smiled and greeted her.

"Father?" Mrs. Winters had a brief frown of confusion immediately replaced by a sigh of relief.

"Please come in, it is very good timing." Mrs. Winters cleared the way for him to enter, and closed the door behind her.

"You have come at the right time; I was wondering if you could help me understand all this." Mrs. Winters said with a trembling voice. She tried really hard to not burst into tears, but she couldn't keep herself for long.

"Oh, Father, I have been through hell…." She sobbed and buried her face in his chest.

"I know," he whispered, looking at the glasses of lemonade.

Mrs. Winters adjusted her shawl that she didn't remember she had on her shoulders. She sniffed and smiled apologetically at the doctor standing in front of her.

"Father, I am sorry, I, uh, I…I messed your coat, oh, look at me, let me get your coat." Mrs. Winters hurriedly helped him take off his coat. She hung it near the main door, and returned to the living room, dreading each moment.

"I am going through a lot," Mrs. Winters said.

"I know," he whispered, looking at the glasses of lemonade.

"I am sorry, I, I just, I am so overwhelmed, Father," Mrs. Winters wiped the perspiration from her brows.

"I can see that," he spoke gently.

"Were you expecting guests?" He asked her.

"What? No, I mean, not at this hour. Oh, but you are most welcome any time, what brings you here?" She was flustered with nervousness.

"We had an appointment today," Dr. Samuel cleared his throat.

"Yes, we had one. I am sorry, I forgot about it." Mrs. Winters smiled apologetically again.

"You didn't. You attended the session." Dr. Samuel looked very calm which was odd, given the situation was nothing short of absolute madness.

"You went out, Stella," Amy spoke from the kitchen counter.

"Oh, yes, I did. I, uh, sorry, I have been through a lot lately," Mrs. Winters gently smacked her forehead and spoke softly.

"It's alright. So, why are there two glasses of lemonade?" Dr. Samuel asked her.

Mrs. Winters didn't respond. She remained silent for a long while, shuddering and muttering something under her breath. Her head hung low as she sat on the sofa, and in a minute, she curled her knees and wrapped herself in an embrace. A thread of drool hung from her mouth which Dr. Samuel observed from where he sat.

"Ich…." Mrs. Winters tried to speak.

"Yes, you what?" Dr. Samuel encouraged her.

"Go on, Stella, tell him." Amy hissed from the same spot she had been standing.

"Ich….I…" Mrs. Winters struggled with her words. Her breathing pattern had changed, and so had her demeanor. She was frigidly twisting her knuckles and swaying her head from left to right.

"You cunt." Mrs. Winters said.

"Don't be like that, Stella, you have to tell him what you did. What you asked us to do, and why we are here." Amy said in a Scottish accent. Her palms were folded one over another, in the exact manner of a royal lady.

"Am I speaking to Mrs. Winters?" Dr. Samuel said slowly. His tone was almost a whisper that reached a minor distance, enough to reach Mrs. Winters' though.

Guttural noise. Creaking and croaking sound from Mrs. Winters.

"Mrs. Winters?" Dr. Samuel looked at her with concern.

"TELL HIM WHAT YOU DID TO HER." Amy yelled.

"I didn't do anything." Mrs. Winters put her hand on her ears and screamed.

"Why did you bury me, mother? Did I not mean anything to you?" Amy said in her own voice. She seemed broken and hurt. Mrs. Winters looked at her and began to cry.

"I…had… no…. choice…" she wept.

"Okay, so tell me, Mrs. Winters." Dr. Samuel intervened.

"I need peace." Mrs. Winters put her hands on her head, and rubbed her temples. She stared on the floor and didn't make eye contact with either Amy, or Dr. Samuel.

"Why did you bury me, mother? Why?" Amy said. It was not a question anymore. It was an objection.

"I didn't kill you. You were already dead." Mrs. Winters said. Her voice broken with pain and agony. How could one kill their own child?

"No, you are wrong. I was not dead." Amy said in a matter-of-factly tone.

CHAPTER 10

WE ALL FALL

DOWN

Dr. Samuel looked hard at the edge of the table in front of him with a blank expression on his face. He was almost ready for what was coming ahead of him: the dirty skeletons in the dirty closet. He took a deep breath and looked at Mrs. Winters.

"Are you ready, Mrs. Winters?" He asked her.

"Huh? Ready? What do you mean ready? Ready for what? Sorry father, I don't understand…. ready?" She looked as if Dr. Samuel had just told her that she was an old and ugly fat man with a beard on her face. She didn't seem to be in touch with the reality at hand; the expression on her face changed to a sudden realization, which was when she figured that she was in her apartment with her possessed daughter and a father to help her deal with the situation.

"Yes, I am." Mrs. Winters replied solemnly. She knew that there had to be another session.

"By the way, I am sorry about my daughter, and she has been acting a bit strange lately. She, uh, she didn't greet you properly, nor did she ask for your blessings. This is Amy, or sometimes, it is Amy," Mrs. Winters' voice had begun to shake, "This is what I was worried about. There are ghosts in her." She whispered.

"Hello, Amy," Dr. Samuel said without looking anywhere other than Mrs. Winters' face.

"Father, you don't understand…" Mrs. Winters began to sob. "I do, I really do." He reassured her.

Mrs. Winters spoke, but her voice came from a deep void of pain and agony.

"I can't lose my daughter; I need to save her," She sobbed.

"Save her? After you killed her?" Amy growled in an angry tone.

"I didn't kill her," Mrs. Winters sobbed some more.

"I need to inject a tranquilizer, Mrs. Winters; it will only be a minor discomfort. Please bear with me. Lie down on the couch, please, and close your eyes. That's good. You will start to feel relaxed in a while." Dr Samuel helped her lie down.

From a distance, Amy's appearance began to fade away, as though she were nothing but a ghost....

Mrs. Winters?

Stella?

Mommy, help me.

Flash. Dead bodies. Flash. Dead cat. Flash. An idol of Baal.

"Mrs. Winters? Can you hear me?"

A voice spoke from the other end.

Mrs. Winters was somewhere in a tunnel that seemed to have no end. It was a wide area with darkness overpowering everything inside it. Her footsteps were light and almost as if she had no weight. The sound of someone calling her name seemed to be coming from a distant land, far, far away from where she was...

I must run to...

"Mother?" Amy's voice rang in her voice.

Amy...

"Mrs. Winters?" Dr Samuel spoke again.

But where was he? Why couldn't Mrs. Winters see him?

"I, I don't know where are you…" she blabbered and groped for something to hold on to, but the void was what must feel like being under the sea at night — the waves of uncertainty and peace hit her at the same time. She was awkwardly feeling anxious for her daughter, yet a cloud of serenity was all over her.

"You are safe here, Mrs. Winters." Dr. Samuel spoke gently.

"Relax, let go of all that is holding you. Mrs. Winters, walk with me…" the serene voice called her.

The tunnel seemed to dissipate and dissolve, just like Amy had a few moments ago.

"There is a garden with red roses, and the weather is mildly warm, with partial clouds and sun. There is a beautiful scent of lilies and daisies all around you. Now, the scent of roses hits your nose, and you're smiling. Walk with me, Mrs. Winters. Walk straight to the castle of old memories."

"It's ugly and dark…" Mrs. Winters cringed and shrunk on the sofa.

"Replace it with a beautiful castle with a jittery white and gold exterior. It belongs to you. You are the resident there with all your memories. Are we ready to step in?" Dr. Samuel asked her gently.

The clouds of peace and bliss suddenly changed to thunder and heavy rain. No longer was it a peaceful day anymore; it appeared to be a disaster before a hurricane. The winds began to howl like merciless wolves out there to devour you; the leaves and the grass beneath her feet had turned pitch black, with a smoky shade of gray around the edges. The castle was now glaring at Mrs. Winters with a mocking smirk on its face.

"Fuck you, Stella, I will fuck you all over again," the castle roared, which was a mixture of the hurricane approaching her, and the winds howling along with the nasty cackling sound of the castle laughing at her.

"You think it's a fairy tale? Don't you?" the castle had turned blood red.

"I am coming to get you…" The castle had now begun to melt like lava and was approaching her. The hurricane was behind Mrs. Winters, and with the molten lava with gigantic arms that could reach thousands of kilometers in a flip of a second, Mrs. Winters wanted nothing but to die.

"Mrs. Winters…." The voice of Dr. Samuel was getting farther and farther.

"No, stay away." She shrieked in utmost horror.

"STAY AWAY!!!!" She screamed this time.

Mrs. Winters….

Mommy…

Mother….

Stella…I am coming to get you … This is not a fairy tale. I AM THE GHOST OF ALL THAT YOU BURIED….AND HERE, WE ALL FALL DOWN…

Why did you bury me, Mother?

You must honor the pact.

The voices…God, please these voices…help me….

The castle, which was now an engulfing thick layer of lava blanket, had almost reached Mrs. Winters. It sang a song that she had often heard from Amy or Patricia, 'Under the water under the sea, how many dead bodies can you see?'

It was hard to tell why that voice sounded more like Amy, or Patricia, or the child. Nothing made sense.

"Mrs. Winters?" Dr. Samuel said.

She jolted upright on the sofa with perspiration covering her like the plague. Her breathing was insanely fast.

"It's now coming to get me; it's not a fairy tale. There is…. a hurricane…I must…my daughter…." Those were the words Mrs. Winters managed to speak before she passed out on the sofa.

CHAPTER 11

THE STRANGE CASE OF

MRS. WINTERS

Mrs. Winters had been lying on the sofa for a time period she could not calculate; for her, it was the abyss, the nothingness, the non-existence of time, matter, and space around her. It was a resting place for her, like the times when the birds would nestle in their habitats before starting off to find food, or like when the predators let their guard down and play with their little ones – entirely free from all worries and thoughts of the materialistic world.

She was in a state of deep relaxation, or so it seemed outwardly. Her mental faculties had retired from the whirlwind of thoughts and disturbing images from her old memories. But what appeared to be a calm, serene situation of a woman sleeping on a sofa was anything but reality.

Dr. Samuel had paid special attention to the case of Mrs. Winters ever since she had started seeing him. It was more than a decade since he had begun treating her, and at times, he was almost confident that she had finally put the past behind her, but the relapses were terrible. Terrible for him and terrible for her. It would become increasingly difficult to deal with the manic episodes and all the catastrophes it brought forth with it. Not something to look forward to.

He had turned the timer off, the one he used to hypnotize his patients and treat them, heal their wounded past, and let the unresolved feelings resurface so he could replace them with happier ones. This was his usual technique, but it had triggered something else in Mrs. Winters and backfired, much to his confusion.

"Mrs. Winters? Are you here with me?" He gently asked her, slightly leaning towards her ear while maintaining a safe distance. The last thing he wanted to do was to terrify her more than she already was. He was very mindful of doing that, so he stood at the end of the sofa and asked her again, "Mrs. Winters? Can you hear me?"

Some mumbling. Nothing comprehensible.

"Mrs. Winters? We need to do this. This is the only way to heal you and get you back to your functioning self."

"I don't…want…go away…" she resisted in a sleepy mood.

"I will take you down to the memory lane, and we will fix all the broken doors and windows, and we will build a beautiful castle for you." He spoke in the same gentle and tender tone of voice as if to soothe her, where physical touch was forbidden. He hoped the tone and words would do the job.

"Ich...." She mumbled in her sleep.

"Yes...you what? Are you cold? Do you want water?" He asked her.

"Ich...werde..."

The voice seemed to gargle in her mouth. It was a strange croaking sound with a lot of bass in it.

"Ich werde dich...."

Silence.

"Ich werde dich töten..." Mrs. Winters had barely finished her warning or proclamation of her intention to kill the poor doctor trying to help her when she sprang to a mighty force and clung to the father's upper body like a python encircling a mouse.

"Let....me...go..." the doctor was struggling for his life. The strength of an old woman was unbelievable for someone her age and health; she had clutched his chest with her knees and landed herself on his shoulders with her arms around his neck.

"Mrs. Winters…" he gasped for air.

"S…T…ELL…AAA," he cried out in pain and desperation.

He tried his best to shake off the crazy lady cackling and laughing at him, groping him tighter and tighter. God knows how did she get that strength.

It was said that when a man was dying, he got a glimpse of all that had happened in his life. For him, the situation was turning white, then grayish white, which was turning into a blackish hue of nothingness.

Was this how it felt like dying?

"Stella! Way to go! Good girl!" Amy clapped and squealed in delight. She danced and swirled towards the dying doctor and sang, "Under the water, under the sea, how many dead bodies can you see?"

Amy roared in laughter, much louder than the capacity of a human being. The living room was now becoming an aftermath of a deadly disaster. Dr. Samuel had tried all in his power to get rid of the crazy woman on him, strangling him to death, but he couldn't.

"Hush now, little one, it's a mockingbird, momma's gonna buy you a brand…" Amy sang to him.

"Isn't he dead yet?" She immediately changed her demeanor, looked at her mother, and glared at the doctor.

"Ich versuche es…" Mrs. Winters croaked with gritted teeth.

"Try harder, then. You are not trying hard enough. Bite him, bite his neck, chop off that flesh or his windpipe, go on, you can do it." Amy cheered in a sing-song voice.

As if in a robotic stance, Mrs. Winters did exactly what her daughter told her to do.

The last bits of life in Dr. Samuel seemed to shred away as his most beloved patient was digging her teeth in his Adam's apple. He felt mild discomfort at first, which was replaced by instant relief since she had stopped strangling him. He took the chance and grabbed her wrists.

"No, Stella, you are not acting yourself." He spoke to her, maintaining fierce eye contact. His neck had red patches where she had tried to choke him and bite his windpipe or the jugular vein itself. Unlike previously, he was not as gentle with her. He spoke with authority and determination.

"I need to sedate you. And you need to behave. You hear me?" He said.

No response.

All the blood vessels in his body had just started to circulate blood and oxygen, which was previously blocked by her – under any circumstances – he would have run away from the house or called an ambulance. But he was so interested in the strange case of Mrs. Winters that he couldn't bring himself to leave or even look away.

He used her case study in one of his lectures, as well as some pictures and voice recordings for reference. The multiple personalities overlapping each other was a typical response of a mother grieving the loss of a child.

"It is a case of black magic," one of his students had raised his hand and immediately came to the conclusion.

"Now, from the looks of it, you may say that this is black magic or some other occult, but it's not." Dr. Samuel cleared his throat in his classroom and continued, "This is a case of a mental disorder where the patient is too scared to face reality."

"I disagree." The student was persistent.

The other half of the class had sided with him, while some remained strongly associated with dark arts. They studied the strange case of Mrs. Winters and pointed out various factors, like the animal sacrifice, the idols found in her home, and the red markings that indicated witchcraft or devil worship.

Dr. Samuel had dusted those ideas like unwanted cobwebs on the frames of his mind.

"One must not think that science is all you need; there are no other possibilities beyond the realm of science." He had remarked at the end of the class.

He was not satisfied. But he lied to everyone that he was. How could he tell them that the very foundations of science and logic that he had always relied on now seemed shaky and…weak? And how on earth could he justify the dead cat in his office? Superhuman? No. The Devil? Maybe. Baal? Highly likely.

"Are you about to piss your pants, father?" Mrs. Winters was sitting in the same spot with a smirk on her face. Her eyes had a darker look in them.

"You scared pussy," she chuckled, with her face darkening every second. Her smile was getting wider and wider with all sorts of creepiness adding to it.

"I am not scared of you," he lied.

"Lügner," she laughed.

"I am not lying." He tried harder.

"You are. Where is your god now?" Mrs. Winters laughed again with her hands up in the air as if to summon more evil in her.

"I AM THE GOD SHE MADE A PACT WITH," her expression changed to a sober and solemn person. It was not Mrs. Winters. It was her body, but the face was that of a devil. The wrinkles had advanced to form layers of unwanted skin hanging loose from her cheeks, her teeth were unusually sharp and long, and her eyes had black hollow sockets around them – all of this was not Mrs. Winters at all. Not the woman who was his favorite patient. The woman he had felt sorry for, the woman he wanted to help no matter what, was no longer in front of him.

"Are you for real?" he whispered. His underarms and forehead had perspiration as if he had stepped out of the gym. He was frozen.

Is this real? Is there a devil after all?

"I am as real as the skin on your nose. I am the god she prayed to, and I brought her daughter back to life. She owes me a lot more than you think, you fool." Mrs. Winters spoke.

"Who are….you…" Dr. Samuel gulped and licked his lips. He regretted his decision to be in that house with Mrs. Winters by himself. He wanted to call the police or anyone who could save him from the devil. But wasn't he a disbeliever? Didn't he refute the ideas of evil and demons?

"I made her do it." Mrs. Winters exclaimed with her eyes wide. The pupils had grown much larger, or so Dr. Samuel thought.

"Do what…." He just moved his lips.

"Kill a life to save a life." She cackled again.

It was Dr. Samuel's turn to pass out.

CHAPTER 12

PUTTING THE PIECES

TOGETHER

Mrs. Winters sat in the cold, sterile room of the mental asylum, her hands trembling slightly as she held onto the edge of the table. The walls around her were stark white, the air thick with the scent of antiseptic. The quiet hum of fluorescent lights filled the silence, but her mind was far from quiet. It raced through the labyrinth of memories, both real and imagined, seeking answers, seeking meaning. She stared at the wall in front of her, her eyes unfocused, as if looking through the veneer of reality and into the depths of a truth she had long been running from.

For years, she had lived in a fog, half in this world and half in the one she had created. The hallucinations, the voices, the strange forces that had taken hold of her—those were not the work of a mind on the brink of collapse. No, they were the product of something much darker, something she had conjured herself. And now, in the quietude of the asylum, the truth was finally becoming clear.

She had always known the pain of losing her daughter, Amy. The accident that had taken her from her had shattered her world in ways words could never describe. Amy had been everything to her, her light, her joy, the reason she got up every morning. And when she had died, something inside Mrs. Winters had broken. But what she hadn't understood then, what she hadn't been able to see, was that Amy hadn't truly died. Not completely.

The accident had left Amy in a coma, hovering on the brink of life and death. But Mrs. Winters, in her grief-stricken desperation, had believed she was gone. And in that moment, in that fragile state of mind, she had made a choice. A choice that would haunt her for the rest of her life.

She had turned to the occult.

In her desperation to bring her daughter back, to defy the cruel hand of fate, Mrs. Winters had sought out the dark arts. She had found an ancient ritual, a ritual that promised to restore life, to bring the dead back to the living, but at a terrible cost. She had been told that the sacrifice required to bring her daughter back was no mere trinket or offering. No, it demanded a life. A heart. A soul.

And so, Mrs. Winters had taken her daughter's life into her own hands.

In the dead of night, under the flickering candlelight of an altar adorned with symbols of power, Mrs. Winters had performed the ritual. She had taken a knife, the blade cold and unforgiving, and with trembling hands, had cut her daughter open. She had removed Amy's heart, the organ that had once beat with love and life, and placed it before the god Baal, offering it as a tribute. She had done this with a belief, a conviction, that Amy would return to her, whole and alive.

But what she hadn't realized, what she had failed to understand in her blind obsession, was that Baal was not a god of mercy. He was a god of darkness, of power, and he did not work in the ways she had hoped. He did not return life to the body he had taken. Instead, he twisted it, contorting it into something monstrous, something that could never truly be called alive. Amy had not returned in the form of the daughter Mrs. Winters had known. No, she had returned as something else—something that wore her face, but was not truly her.

It was the horror of this realization that had driven Mrs. Winters to madness. She had believed her daughter was dead, had mourned her as one mourns the loss of a loved one. But

Amy had never truly died. And in her misguided attempt to bring her back, Mrs. Winters had created a monster.

The hallucinations had started soon after. Amy—no, Stella, the creature that wore her skin—had begun to appear to Mrs. Winters, whispering to her, calling her to do things, to perform rituals. The dark god had demanded his due, and Mrs. Winters had been forced to obey. She had given up pieces of herself, her sanity, her soul, until there was nothing left but the hollow shell of a woman who no longer recognized the world around her.

But now, in the sterile confines of the asylum, Mrs. Winters understood. She understood that she had been living in a nightmare of her own making. The creature that had tormented her, the one she had called Amy, was not her daughter. It was a twisted reflection of the bargain she had made with Baal, a reflection of her guilt, her grief, and her madness. And the hallucinations, the voices, the terrifying visions, they were all part of the price she had paid.

Her mind had fractured under the weight of it all. The once-well-ordered thoughts of a mother had splintered into a chaotic storm of guilt, sorrow, and terror. She had been trapped in that storm for years, unable to escape, unable to see the truth. But now, finally, the fog was lifting.

The door to her room opened, and a nurse stepped inside, her face soft and sympathetic. Mrs. Winters didn't even look up, her eyes still fixed on the wall in front of her. She had been expecting this. The nurse approached her slowly, gently, as if afraid of disturbing her fragile state.

"Mrs. Winters," the nurse said softly, "Now it's time for your medication."

Mrs. Winters blinked, her mind slowly returning to the present. She had grown accustomed to the routine, to the endless cycle of sedatives and therapy, but it all felt so hollow now. She had spent so long trying to quiet the voices, to numb the memories, but no amount of medication could erase the truth. It was there, deep inside her, like a dark seed that had taken root in her soul.

"I don't need the medication," Mrs. Winters whispered, her voice hoarse and raspy. "I already know."

The nurse paused, confused. "Know what, Mrs. Winters?"

Mrs. Winters turned her gaze to the nurse, her eyes wide and wild, but there was a clarity in them now, a recognition of the truth that had eluded her for so long. "I know what I did," she said, her voice trembling with the weight of her confession. "I know what I became."

The nurse recoiled slightly, unsure of what to say. Mrs. Winters continued, her voice growing stronger with each word.

"I killed her," she said, her eyes filling with tears. "I killed my own daughter."

The nurse stepped back, alarmed. "Mrs. Winters, we've talked about this before. You need to calm down. You're not in control of your thoughts right now."

But Mrs. Winters shook her head. "No, I'm not crazy," she said, her voice breaking. "I did it. I killed her. And I brought something else back. Something terrible."

The nurse looked at her, unsure of how to respond. She had heard the stories, the rumors, the whispers about Mrs. Winters and her strange behavior, but she had never fully understood them. Now, as she looked into the woman's eyes, she saw something there—a glimpse of the terror that had gripped her for so long.

"Please, let me help you," the nurse said softly, reaching out to touch her arm. "We can help you get better."

Mrs. Winters pulled away from her touch, her eyes wide with panic. "No," she whispered. "There's no fixing this. It's too late."

The door to the room opened again, and a doctor entered. He was a young man, clean-cut, with a look of concern on his face. "How's she doing?" he asked the nurse.

"She's... she's finally talking about it," the nurse said, her voice uncertain. "She's saying she killed her daughter."

The doctor nodded, his expression unreadable. "It's good that she's acknowledging it. That's the first step."

But Mrs. Winters shook her head, her eyes wild. "It's too late," she whispered again, her voice barely audible. "I can never undo what I did."

The doctor leaned closer to her. "You don't have to undo anything, Mrs. Winters. You just need to let us help you. We can work through this together."

But Mrs. Winters only stared at him, her eyes filled with a deep, haunting sadness. "There's nothing left to fix," she said softly. "I've already lost everything."

And in that moment, in the quiet of the asylum room, the weight of Mrs. Winters' realization pressed down on her. She had killed her daughter, not with her hands, but with her desperation, with her belief that she could control life and death. And in the end, she had destroyed everything she had ever loved.

The darkness that had gripped her mind, the hallucinations, the voices—those were the echoes of the ritual, the curse she had brought upon herself. And now, there was no escape. There was no redemption.

In the silence of the room, Mrs. Winters felt a wave of relief wash over her. She had finally faced the truth. She had finally understood the price she had paid.

But that knowledge, that terrible truth, was the last thing she would ever hold onto. And as she closed her eyes, the darkness that had once consumed her mind now seemed to envelop her entirely, taking her into its embrace.

www.ingramcontent.com/pod-product-compliance
Lightning Source LLC
Chambersburg PA
CBHW022159150726
47992CB00002B/867